ELAN, SON OF TWO PEOPLES

FOR DAVID AND JOANNA
—*H.S.H.*

TO MY FAMILY
—*M.P.*

Text copyright © 2014 by Heidi Smith Hyde
Illustrations copyright © 2014 by Lerner Publishing Group

Kar-Ben Publishing
A division of Lerner Publishing Group, Inc.
241 First Avenue North
Minneapolis, MN 55401 U.S.A.

Website address: www.karben.com

Main body text set in Claude Sans Std 17/21.
Typeface provided by International Typeface Corp.

Library of Congress Cataloging-in-Publication Data

Hyde, Heidi Smith.
    Elan, son of two peoples / by Heidi Smith Hyde ; illustrated by Mikela Prevost.
       pages   cm
    Summary: In 1898, just after his Bar Mitzvah, thirteen-year-old Elan and his family travel to Albuquerque, New Mexico, where he meets his mother's family and participates in the Pueblo ceremony of becoming a man.
    ISBN 978-0-7613-9051-0 (lib. bdg. : alk. paper)
    ISBN 978-1-4677-2430-2 (eBook)
    [1. Coming of age—Fiction. 2. Jews—United States—Fiction. 3. Pueblo Indians—Fiction. 4. Indians of North America—New Mexico—Fiction. 5. New Mexico—History—19th century—Fiction.] I. Prevost, Mikela, illustrator. II. Title.
PZ7.H9677El 2014
[E]—dc23   2013002190

Manufactured in the United States of America
1 - PC - 7/15/13

ELAN, SON OF TWO PEOPLES

HEIDI SMITH HYDE   ILLUSTRATED BY MIKELA PREVOST

KAR-BEN
PUBLISHING

Elan watched from his window as the city of San Francisco faded into the distance. It was 1898, and he and his family were on a railway journey which would take them all the way to Albuquerque, New Mexico.

"You won't be seeing fancy new cable cars where we're headed, Elan," his father told him. "Just dusty, old frontier towns and an endless stretch of desert."

Elan never imagined turning thirteen would be so exciting. Only yesterday, he had been called to the Torah as a Bar Mitzvah. Wearing his grandfather's tallit, he had chanted from the portion called *Bamidbar,* which tells of the Jewish people wandering in the desert. Now he was going to see what an American desert was like.

And he would finally get to see the place where his mother was born. Mama, or Naya, as Elan called her, was the granddaughter of a Pueblo Indian chief.

Papa, the son of a cantor, emigrated to New Mexico from Eastern Europe. There he opened a trading post where he sold tools, blankets, kettles, and glass beads to Naya's tribe.

Elan knew that when he turned thirteen he would have two celebrations. In addition to his Bar Mitzvah, he would take part in the Pueblo ceremony of becoming a man. This celebration would take place on the mesa, the flat-topped mountain range where Mama and Papa first met.

As the train chugged down the tracks, his mother handed him a small package. "For your Bar Mitzvah you wore your grandfather's tallit. But on Shabbat when you read Torah for my family, you can wear this."

"My own tallit!" Elan exclaimed with delight. "So this is the surprise you've been weaving all summer!"

"In my culture the men do most of the weaving, but I learned this skill from your grandfather," his mother said proudly.

Each end of the tallit had colorful stripes; yellow for the sun, blue for the corn, white for the rocks, and red for Mother Earth. Pale green fringes, like shimmering blades of grass, were tied to the corners.

Woven between the stripes were four symbols; a Star of David, the Ten Commandments, a stalk of corn, and an oak tree.

"I know why the tree is there, Naya," Elan said. "It's because my name means 'oak tree' in Hebrew!"

"Yes," his mother said, "but there's another reason. In the language of my people, 'Elan' means 'friendly.' Always remember you are the son of two proud nations, whose roots are as sturdy and deep as this oak tree.

"And the corn stalk is there because every year on the mesa we have a ceremony to pray for rain and give thanks for the harvest. Women grind corn on slabs of stone, while the men play drums and sing songs of praise. It was at the Corn Festival that I first met your father."

"Tell me again what happened," Elan asked.

His mother smiled softly. "Papa and I married, but first I became a member of the Jewish community. We moved to San Francisco when you were just a baby."

As their journey continued, Elan and his family passed through many frontier towns. In Snake Canyon, they ate peppermint candy and drank sarsaparilla at the general store.

In Dry Gulch, he watched the sheriff haul a prisoner off to the jailhouse.

In Silverton, he saw a blacksmith shoeing a horse.

Finally the train reached Albuquerque. From there the family took a horse and wagon to the mesa.

"It's so high up you can touch the clouds," Elan said, marveling at his first look at the majestic landscape.

That evening, Elan stayed in an adobe house, a two-story structure made of clay. For dinner he ate a delicious meal of soup, baked beans, and cornbread. Afterwards, he went to sleep on a sheepskin rug.

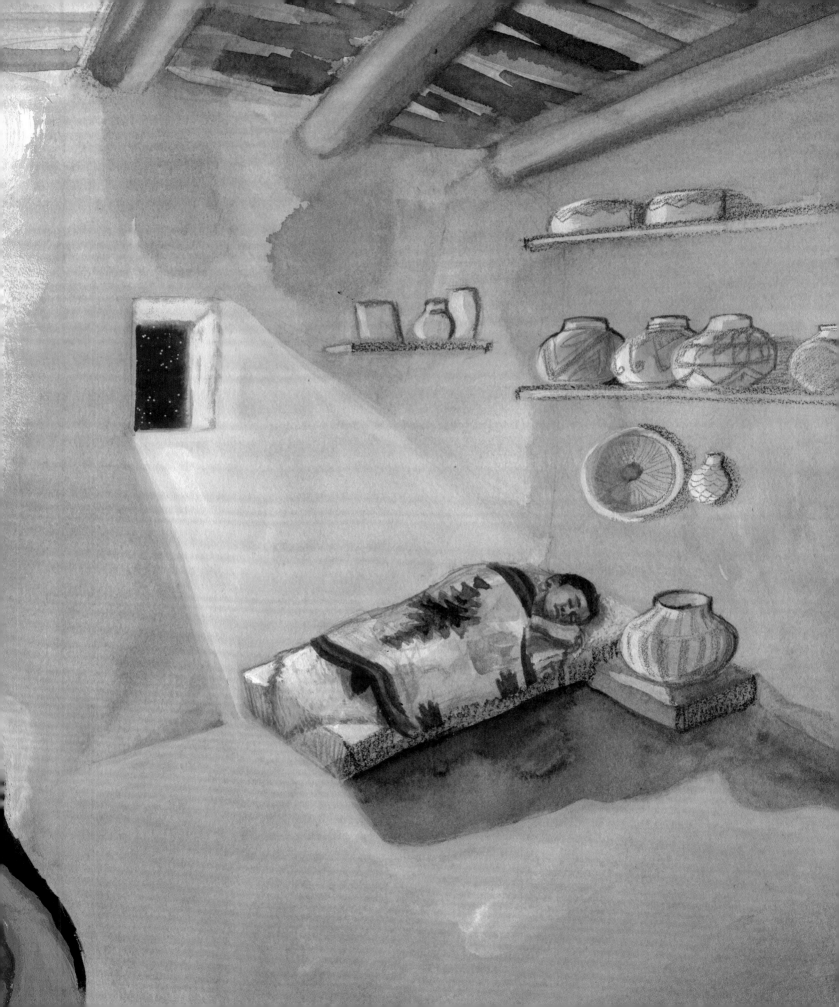

The next morning he met his cousin Manolo, and together they roamed the rocky mesa. There was so much to do and see. At night they crowded around the fireplace while their grandfather told stories, beginning with the words *hum-ah-ha* or "long, long ago."

When Shabbat came, Elan, his parents, and his Indian family gathered on the mesa beneath a canopy of blue sky. Manolo gazed curiously at the small Torah Elan had brought with him on the train. Elan told him about becoming a Bar Mitzvah.

"Soon you will become an adult member of the Acoma Pueblo as well," Manolo whispered. "Then we can go hunting and fishing with the men."

Carefully, Elan opened the Torah and placed it on a ledge of solid rock. Wrapping himself in his new tallit, he began to chant in a clear, confident voice.

When all the prayers and blessings had been said, the tribal chief approached him with an outstretched hand. "Tonight you will become an Acoma tribesman," he said solemnly.

After sundown Elan dressed in a tunic, leggings, and deerskin moccasins. Then he and his father followed the elders to the *kiva,* a Pueblo ceremonial room. Elan wished his mother could come along too, but only men were allowed to take part in the rituals.

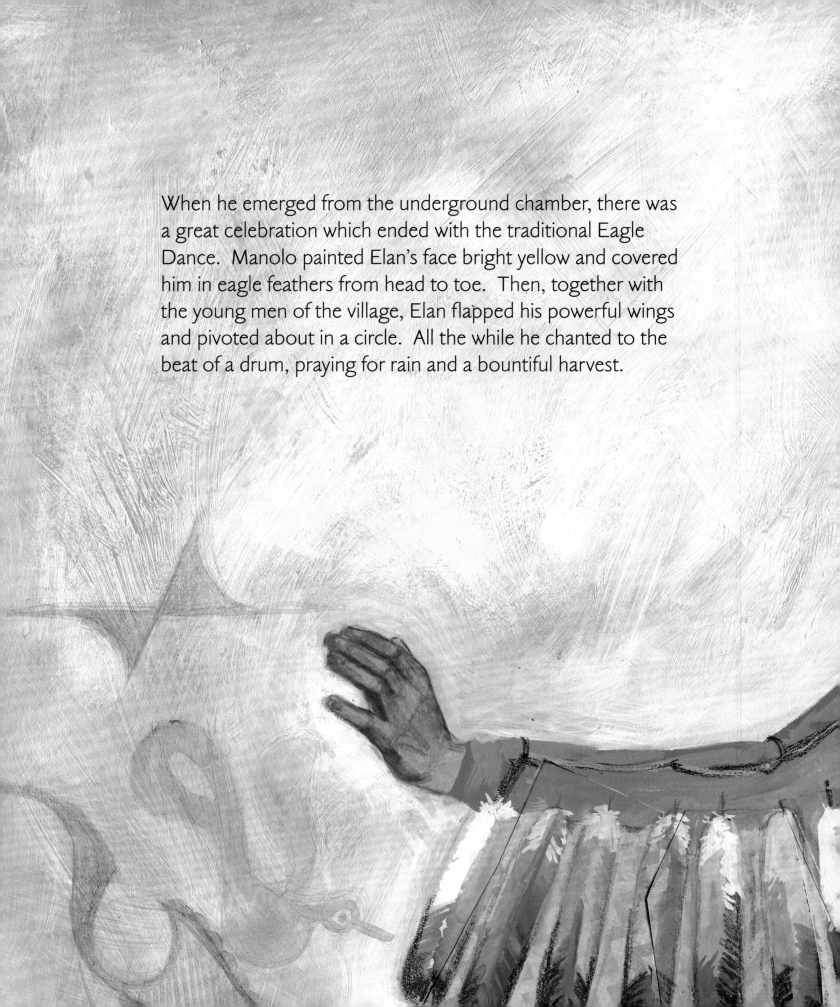

When he emerged from the underground chamber, there was a great celebration which ended with the traditional Eagle Dance. Manolo painted Elan's face bright yellow and covered him in eagle feathers from head to toe. Then, together with the young men of the village, Elan flapped his powerful wings and pivoted about in a circle. All the while he chanted to the beat of a drum, praying for rain and a bountiful harvest.

Elan's prayers were answered. The very next day a cooling rain came. He spent the afternoon with Manolo, exploring remote caves and waterfalls. The day after that, they went trout fishing with the men along the riverbank.

"I will miss this place," said Elan when his last day on the mesa arrived.

"I hope you will come back again next year," Manolo said. "Then we will go camping in the mountains."

Before returning home to San Francisco, Elan packed his tunic, leggings, and moccasins. Then he packed the eagle feathers next to his small Torah. As he placed his tallit bag on top, he looked again at the Star of David, the Ten Commandments, the stalk of corn, and the oak tree.

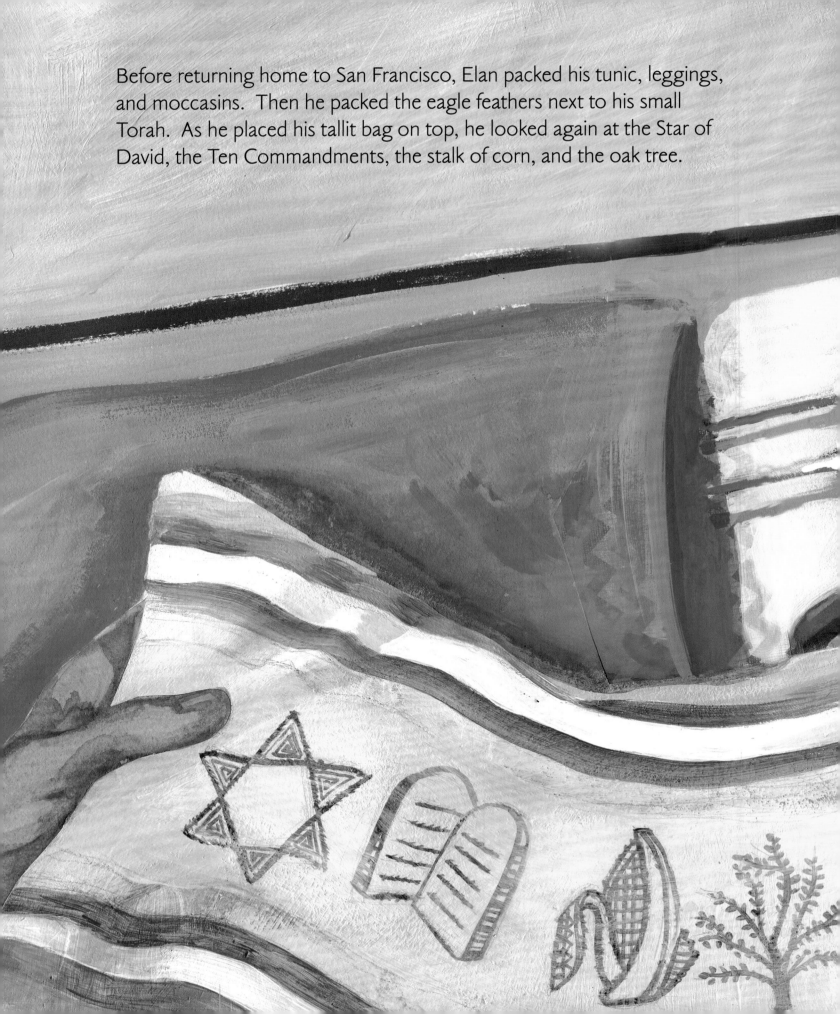

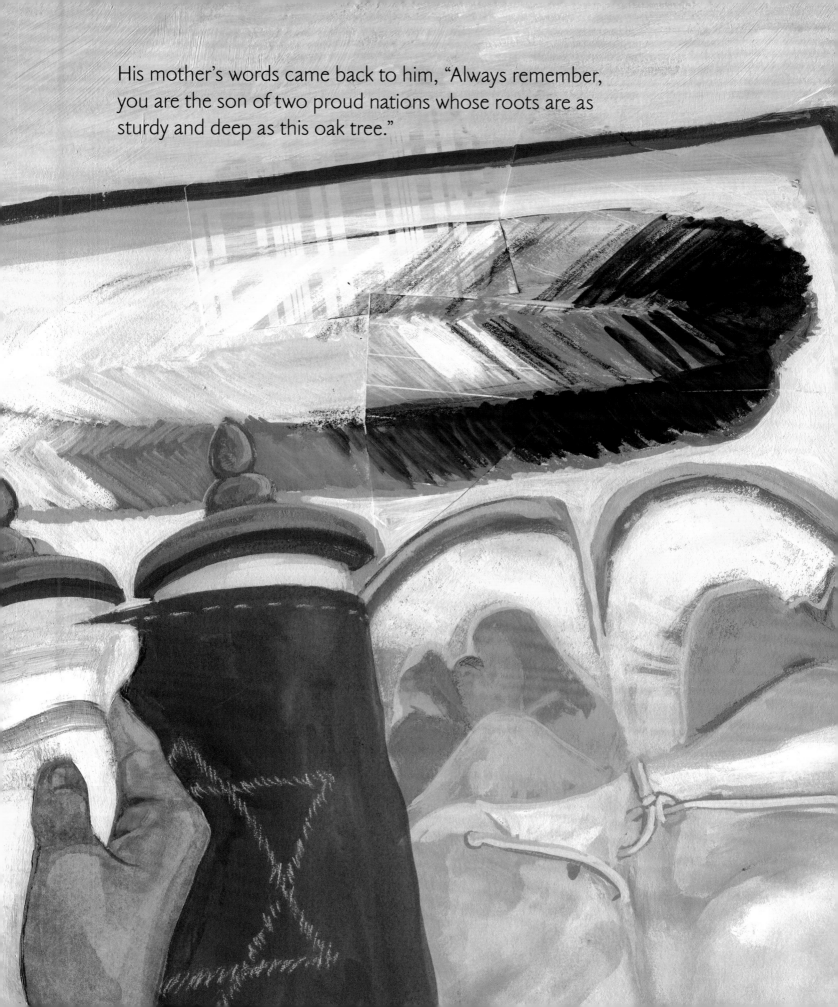

His mother's words came back to him, "Always remember, you are the son of two proud nations whose roots are as sturdy and deep as this oak tree."

Historical note

While many East European Jewish immigrants settled in New York, some ventured west to seek their fortune. They found work as peddlers, traders, prospectors, and storekeepers. One such adventurer was Solomon Bibo, whose life inspired this story. Bibo was 16 years old when he immigrated from Prussia to New Mexico in 1869 to join his brothers' mercantile business. Fascinated with Native American culture, Solomon opened a trading post atop a mesa and became fluent in the Keres language. In 1885, he married Juana Valle, granddaughter of a former Acoma Pueblo chief. Juana is assumed to have converted to Judaism although, in the fluid environment of the West at that time, a rabbi was often not available. The couple lived a Jewish life and raised their children as Jews.

Later Bibo was appointed Pueblo governor, the Acoma equivalent of a tribal chief. An outspoken advocate for Native American rights, he worked tirelessly to secure more land for the Pueblo. At the turn of the century, he and his wife moved to San Francisco to provide for their children's Jewish education. In addition to becoming a Bar Mitzvah, their eldest son participated in the Acoma rituals of manhood. Both Solomon Bibo and his wife Juana are buried in a Jewish cemetery in California.

Glossary

Bamidbar: "In the Desert," one of the weekly Torah portions

Bar Mitzvah: Coming-of-age ceremony for Jewish boys, held at age 13

Cantor: Person who leads the singing and prayers during Jewish religious services

Sarsaparilla: A sweetened soft drink similar to root beer

Tallit: Jewish prayer shawl

Torah: The "Five Books of Moses" read from a scroll in synagogue

Heidi Smith Hyde is the Director of Education of Temple Sinai in Brookline, MA. Her books include *Feivel's Flying Horses*, a National Jewish Book Award Finalist, *Mendel's Accordion*, winner of the Sugarman Award for Best Jewish Children's Book, and *Emanuel and the Hanukah Rescue*. She and her family live in Chestnut Hill, Massachusetts.

Mikela Prevost is fascinated by people and often sketches her friends, who then find themselves in one of her books. She received her B.A. in Painting and Drawing from the University of Redlands and her M.F.A. in Illustration from Cal State Fullerton. She and her family live in Peoria, AZ.